STEP-BY-STEP EXPERIMENTS WITH MATTER

By Gina Hagler

Illustrated by Bob Ostrom

The Child's World

Published by The Child's World®
1980 Lookout Drive • Mankato, MN 56003-1705
800-599-READ • www.childsworld.com

ACKNOWLEDGMENTS
The Child's World®: Mary Berendes, Publishing Director
The Design Lab: Design and production
Red Line Editorial: Editorial direction
Consultant: Dr. Peter Barnes, Assistant Scientist, Astronomy Dept.,
   University of Florida

ISBN 9781609735906
LCCN 2011940145

PHOTO CREDITS
Andrey Armyagov/Dreamstime, cover; Pilar Echeverria/Dreamstime,
cover, back cover; Robisklp/Dreamstime, 1, 31; Shutterstock Images, 4,
8, 12, 21; Ross Aaron Everhard/Shutterstock Images, 16; iStockphoto,
24; Piotr Kozikowski/Dreamstime, 26; Sarunez/Dreamstime, 28

Design elements: Pilar Echeverria/Dreamstime, Robisklp/Dreamstime,
Jeffrey Van Daele/Dreamstime, Sarit Saliman/Dreamstime

Printed in the United States of America

BE SAFE !

The experiments in this book are meant for kids to do themselves. Sometimes an adult's help is needed though. Look in the supply list for each experiment. It will list if an adult is needed. Also, some supplies will need to be bought by an adult.

TABLE OF CONTENTS

4

Air, water, and mountains are made from different states of matter.

CHAPTER ONE

Study Matter!

Do you wonder what makes liquids freeze? What about gases? Do you wonder if you can touch or see them? These things have something in common. They are states of matter. Everything around you is made of matter. You are made of matter. The air is made of matter. The leaves on trees are made of matter, too. Some matter can be seen and touched. Other matter is hard to sense. It often has no smell or color.

There are three main states of matter. Matter can be solid, like the soil in a flowerpot. It can be liquid, like the water in a river. Or it can be a gas, like the air we breathe. There is a fourth type of matter, too. It is called a plasma. Plasma is found in the sun and the stars. It is also what glows inside neon signs. How can you learn more about matter?

CHAPTER TWO

Seven Science Steps

Doing a science **experiment** is a fun way to discover new facts.
An experiment follows steps to find answers to science questions.
This book has experiments to help you learn about matter.
You will follow the same seven steps in each experiment:

Seven Steps

1. Research: Figure out the facts before you get started.

2. Question: What do you want to learn?

3. Guess: Make a **prediction**. What do you think will happen in the experiment?

4. Gather: Find the supplies you need for your experiment.

5. Experiment: Follow the directions.

6. Review: Look at the results of the experiment.

7. Conclusion: The experiment is done. Now it is time to reach a **conclusion**. Was your prediction right?

Are you ready to become a scientist? Let's experiment to learn about matter!

Ice keeps drinks cold.

CHAPTER THREE

Ice and Heat

Ice keeps your drink cold. But what happens to it after a while? It melts into the drink. What makes ice change its state? Try this experiment to find out.

Research the Facts

Here are a few. Can you find some more?

- Ice is water in a solid state.
- Cold temperatures make ice freeze.

Ask Questions

- What happens to ice when it is heated?
- Does sunlight heat ice?

Make a Prediction

Here are two examples:

- Ice stays solid in the heat and cold.
- Ice melts into a liquid in the heat.

- 2 clear cups
- Ice cubes
- Sunlight
- Clock
- Pencil or pen
- Paper

Time to Experiment!

1. Put two ice cubes in each cup.
2. Look at the ice in the cup. What does it look like? Write down what you see.
3. Place one cup in the sunlight. Place the other cup in a shady spot.
4. Leave the cups alone for 30 minutes.

10

5. Take a look at the ice again. What happened in each cup? Write down what you see.

Review the Results

Read your notes. Did the ice in the cups change? The ice melted in both cups. There is more liquid in the cup that was in the sunlight.

What Is Your Conclusion?

Did you predict the right answer? Ice changes into a liquid when it is heated. The sunlight's warmth made the ice melt. The ice cubes melted faster in the sunlight. This made more liquid appear in this cup. The cup in the shady spot did not get as hot. Less liquid was in the cup. Ice needs heat to change its state to liquid.

12

Frost covers windows in the winter.

So Frosty!

Water can also be a gas. It is in the air around us all the time. When it gets cold enough, what happens to the water? Try this to find out!

Research the Facts

Here are a few facts. What can you find in your research?

- **Water vapor** is water that is in the form of gas.
- Frost is a solid state of water.
- Frost returns to a liquid state when heated.

Ask Questions

- What happens to water vapor in cold temperatures?
- Where does frost come from?

Make a Prediction

Here are two examples:

- The water vapor will stay in the air.
- The water vapor will turn into a liquid.

Gather Your Supplies!

- Empty metal food can
- Teaspoon
- Ice
- Salt
- Pencil or pen
- Paper

Time to Experiment!

1. Put 3 teaspoons of salt into the can.
2. Fill the can halfway with ice.
3. Add another 3 teaspoons of salt.
4. Add more ice until the can is almost filled.

5. Add another 3 teaspoons of salt.

6. Stir the ice and salt with the spoon for about one minute.

7. Remove the spoon and wait five minutes.

8. Record your observations. What happened to the outside of the can?

Review the Results

Did you predict the right answer? The can is very cold. Liquid and frost appeared on the outside of the can.

What Is Your Conclusion?

There was water vapor in the air around the can. It changed state from a gas to a liquid. On the cold can, some of the liquid turned to a solid. This solid is frost.

CHAPTER FIVE

Where's the Salt?

Water **evaporates** when it is heated. But what happens to solids in the water when it evaporates? This experiment will show you.

Research the Facts

Here are a few facts. What other facts can you find?

- Some solids **dissolve** in water, such as sugar and salt. The solid spreads evenly in the liquid. It looks like the solid disappears.
- Solids in a liquid make a **solution**.
- Water evaporates if it is left in sunlight.

Salt is a solid that can dissolve into liquid.

16

Ask Questions

- Where does salt go when salty water evaporates?
- Can a solid separate from a solution?

Make a Prediction

Here are two examples:

- Water and solids in a solution evaporate.
- Water in a solution evaporates, but solids are left behind.

Gather Your Supplies!

- Rimmed tray
- Measuring cup
- Water
- Salt
- Tablespoon
- Sunlight
- Black construction paper
- Pencil or pen
- Paper

Time to Experiment!

1. Fill the measuring cup with water to the $^1/_2$ mark.

2. Add 3 tablespoons of salt to the water. Stir the salt until it dissolves.

3. Put the black paper on the tray.

4. Pour the salty water over the paper in the tray.

5. Look at the water in the tray. Write down what you see.
6. Place the tray by a sunny window.
7. Leave your experiment alone for seven days. Put it in a place it will not be bumped or moved.
8. Look in the tray. Do you see anything? Record what you see.

Review the Results

What did you observe? What happened to the water in the tray? What is left on the paper? The water evaporated. But the salt did not evaporate. Salt **crystals** were left behind on the paper.

What Is Your Conclusion?

When water is heated it evaporates. The heat from the sun makes water **molecules** move faster. As they move faster, they become a gas. The evaporated water goes into the air around you. The solids in the water are left behind. The solids cannot turn into a gas. The salt sticks together to make crystals.

All matter is made of tiny parts called molecules. In different temperatures, molecules move at different speeds. In gas, molecules move very fast. In solids, they are much slower.

CHAPTER SIX

Gassy Balloon

A gas is a state of matter that is difficult to see or touch. But gas can fill a container. What happens to gas in a balloon? Try this and see.

Research the Facts

Here are a few facts. What else did you find out about gas?

- Most gases have no smell or color.
- Some solids combine with liquids to make a gas.

Ask Questions

- Can a balloon be filled with gas?
- Can gases be made from a solution?

How do balloons fill up?

21

Make a Prediction

Here are two examples:

- Gas will not fill the balloon.
- Gas will fill the balloon.

Gather Your Supplies!

- A small clear bottle with a narrow neck
- Measuring cup
- Vinegar
- Water
- Baking soda
- Funnel
- Balloon
- Pencil or pen
- Paper

Time to Experiment!

1. Pour about 2 ounces (60 mL) of vinegar into the bottle.

2. Pour about 2 ounces (60 mL) of water into the bottle.

3. Use the funnel to fill the balloon half full with baking soda.

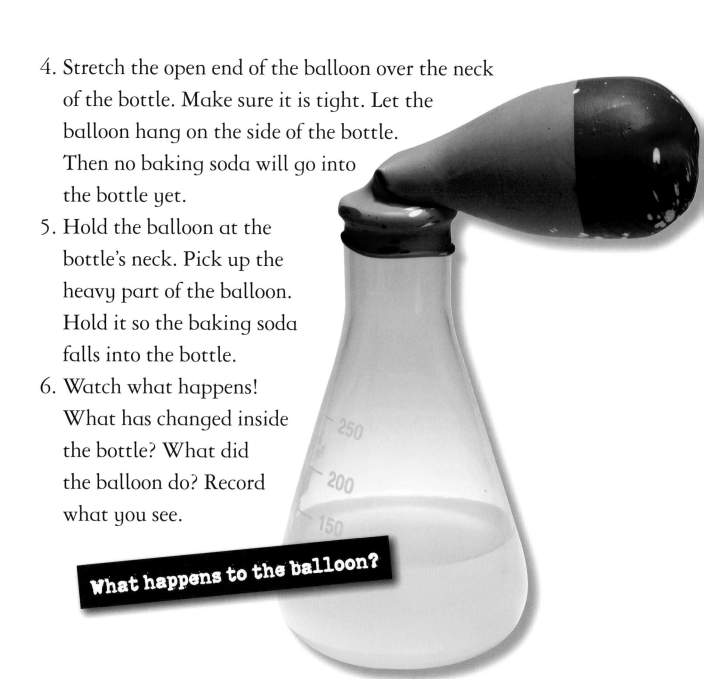

4. Stretch the open end of the balloon over the neck of the bottle. Make sure it is tight. Let the balloon hang on the side of the bottle. Then no baking soda will go into the bottle yet.

5. Hold the balloon at the bottle's neck. Pick up the heavy part of the balloon. Hold it so the baking soda falls into the bottle.

6. Watch what happens! What has changed inside the bottle? What did the balloon do? Record what you see.

What happens to the balloon?

Review the Results

What happened? The mixture in the bottle fizzed and made bubbles. Then the balloon became big and round.

What Is Your Conclusion?

The water, vinegar, and baking soda made a gas when they were mixed. The gas rose from the bottle. It filled up the balloon. The gas took on the shape of the balloon. Gases take the shape of the space they fill. This space can be a container such as a balloon.

Have you had a balloon that floats in the air? That balloon was filled with helium gas. Helium is lighter than air. This makes the balloon float!

CHAPTER SEVEN

Which Freezes Faster?

There are many kinds of liquids. Sometimes liquids become solids. What makes liquids become solids? Try this to find out.

Research the Facts

Here are a few facts. What else can you discover?

- Most liquids change state when they are cooled.
- The freezing point of water is 32° Fahrenheit (0° Celsius).

How fast does milk freeze?

Ask Questions

- Why do some liquids freeze faster than others?
- What happens when liquids become solids?

Make a Prediction

Here are two examples:

- Milk will freeze slowly.
- Milk will freeze faster than many other liquids.

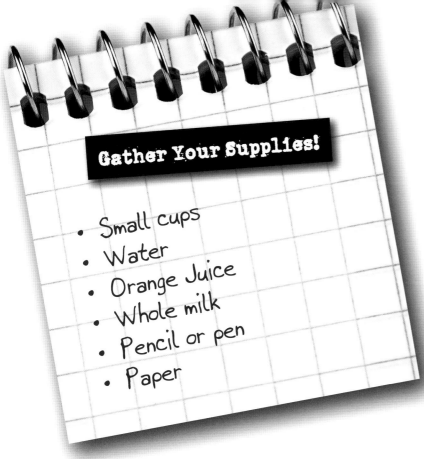

Gather Your Supplies!

- Small cups
- Water
- Orange Juice
- Whole milk
- Pencil or pen
- Paper

Time to Experiment!

1. Fill each cup about half full with one liquid.
2. Look at each liquid. What color is it? Is it hard or easy to see through? Write down what you see.
3. Place all of the cups in the freezer.

4. Check on the cups every ten minutes. Are the liquids frozen? Which ones are frozen?

5. Record what you see. Which liquid froze first? Which one froze last?

Review the Results

Read your notes. Did you see that the liquids froze at different times? The water froze first. And the other liquids froze later.

What Is Your Conclusion?

Different liquids freeze at different temperatures. This is their freezing point. When a liquid freezes, its molecules slow down. This makes the liquid change state. It turns into a solid.

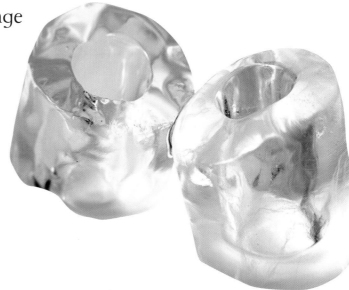

You are a scientist now. What fun matter facts did you learn? You found out that the states of matter include gases, liquids, and solids. You saw that matter can change states. You can learn even more about matter. Study it. Experiment with it. Then share what you learn about matter.

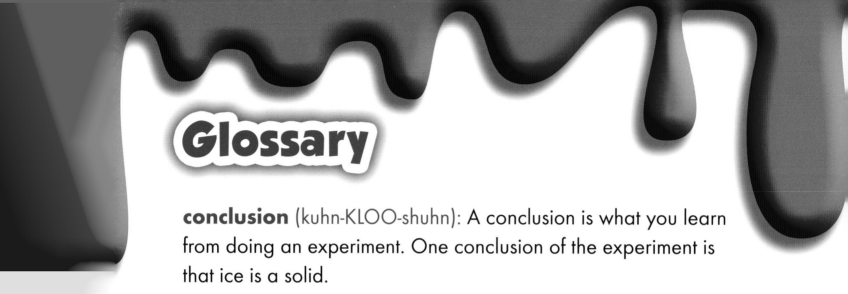

Glossary

conclusion (kuhn-KLOO-shuhn): A conclusion is what you learn from doing an experiment. One conclusion of the experiment is that ice is a solid.

crystals (KRISS-tuhlz): Crystals are a body with many flat surfaces that form when a liquid becomes a solid. Salt formed crystals in an experiment.

dissolve (di-ZOLV): To dissolve is to seem to disappear when mixed with a liquid. Sugar can dissolve in water.

evaporates (i-VAP-uh-rates): Water evaporates when it moves into the air as water vapor. When water evaporates, it becomes a gas.

experiment (ek-SPER-uh-ment): An experiment is a test or way to study something to learn facts. This experiment shows how matter can change its state.

molecules (MOL-uh-kyoolz): Molecules are the smallest part of a substance. Molecules move very fast in a gas.

prediction (pri-DIKT-shun): A prediction is what you think will happen in the future. The prediction for the gas experiment was right.

solution (suh-LOO-shuhn): A solution is a mixture made of a solid or gas that has been dissolved in a liquid. The solution was made from salt and vinegar.

states (STAYTZ): States are the forms a thing, such as water, takes. There are different states of matter.

water vapor (WAW-tur VAY-pur): Water vapor is water in the air that cannot be seen. Steam is water vapor.

Books

Monroe, Tilda. *What Do You Know About States of Matter?* New York: PowerKids Press, 2011.

Robinson, Tom. *The Everything Kids' Science Experiments Book: Boil Ice, Float Water, Measure Gravity-Challenge the World Around You!* Avon, MA: Adams Media, 2001.

Tocci, Salvatore. *Experiments With Solids, Liquids, and Gases.* New York: Children's Press, 2002.

Web Sites

Visit our Web site for links about matter experiments:
childsworld.com/links

Note to Parents, Teachers, and Librarians: We routinely verify our Web links to make sure they are safe and active sites. So encourage your readers to check them out!

Index

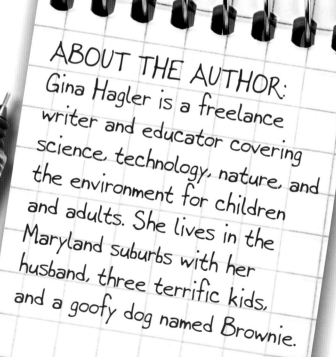

ABOUT THE AUTHOR:
Gina Hagler is a freelance writer and educator covering science, technology, nature, and the environment for children and adults. She lives in the Maryland suburbs with her husband, three terrific kids, and a goofy dog named Brownie.